For my mom,
her mom,
and Rufus

Cori Doerrfeld

GOOD DOG

HARPER

An Imprint of HarperCollinsPublishers

Stray dog.

Lost dog.

Scared dog.

Lonely dog.

Hungry dog.

Sad dog.

Hopeful dog.

Search dog.

Lucky dog.

Happy dog.

Smart dog.

Quick dog.

Brave dog.

Patient dog.

Thoughtful dog.

Careful dog.

Gentle dog.

Loyal dog.

Barking dog.

Rescue dog.

Friendly dog.

Loving dog.

Library of Congress Control Number: 2017943431

ISBN 978-0-06-266286-6

The artist used digital ink to create the illustrations for this book.

Book design by Alison Donalty

18 19 20 21 22   SCP   10 9 8 7 6 5 4 3 2 1

❖ First Edition